hucket-a-bucket

down
the
street

For Michael who had the idea

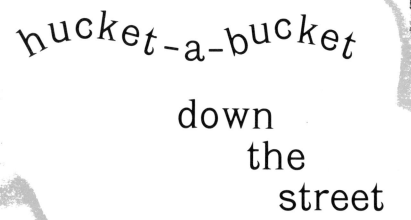

hucket-a-bucket

down
the
street

By Sarah Rush

Illustrated by Howard Kodner

Published by
Lerner Publications Company
Minneapolis, Minnesota

Standard Book Number: 8225-0254-2.
Library of Congress Catalog Number: 64-8403.

Printed in U.S.A. Published simultaneously
in Canada by J. M. Dent & Sons Ltd., Don Mills, Ontario.

Second Printing 1967
Third Printing 1969

Did you ever hear of
the automobile that
went
hucket-a-bucket
down the street?

There was such a car once.

Its name was ANDREW.

Andrew had been built a long time ago —
when the milkman had a horse and wagon
and an iceman brought huge blocks of ice
for people to keep their food cold.

When Andrew was a NEW car, his owner
liked to drive him.

In the summer he drove Andrew
out into the sunshine of the day,
hucket-a-bucket down the street.

Sometimes he tried to run a race
with the moon at night,
hucket-a-bucket down the street.

In the winter Andrew's owner sat snug and warm inside while the snowflakes gently fell on Andrew's hood.

In the spring he let
the raindrops wash
Andrew clean.

After a while, Andrew wasn't new
any more.
His owner drove to a garage for
used cars and left Andrew there!

Was Andrew all used up?
No. His engine had power enough
to go for thousands of miles.
Had Andrew been smashed in an
accident?

No. His steel body was
as strong as a bulldozer.
Then why was Andrew
left in the garage?
His owner wanted a new
car. Andrew had been sold.

Nobody came to drive
Andrew. A spider spun a
web across his windows.
And dust covered him
like a blanket.

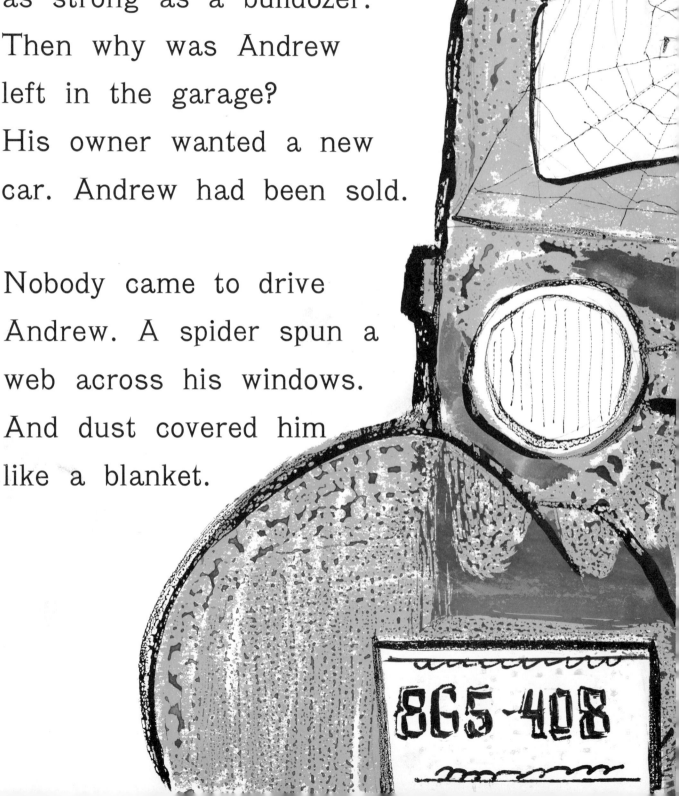

865-408

One day, after a long time passed, something
happened. Three boys raced into the garage.

The first one asked,

"Where is it?"

The second one

shouted,

"Me first!"

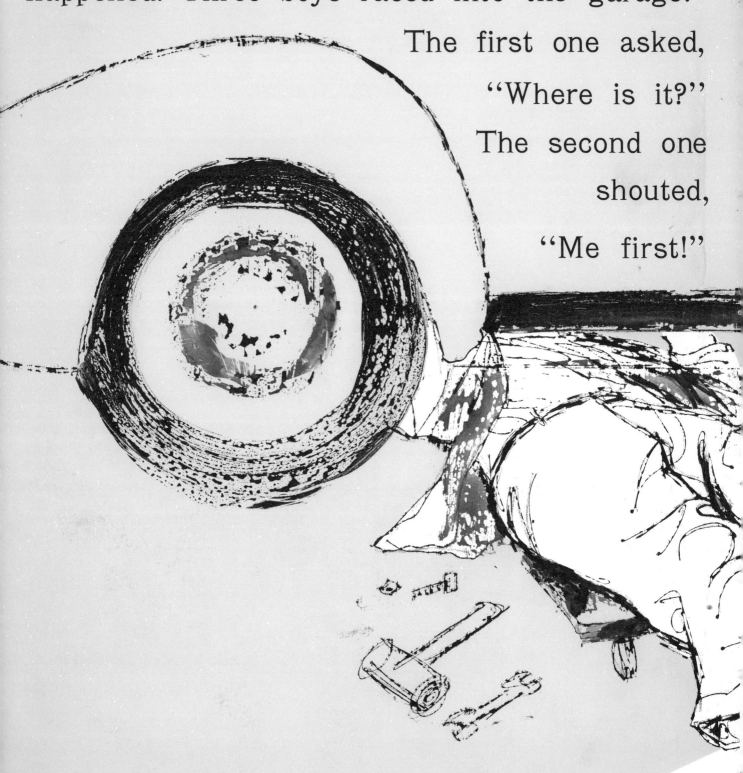

The third one cried, "No, me." Then they all said together, rather politely, "We want to see an OLD car." Their mother and father came huffing and puffing, trying to catch up with the little boys.

The tallest boy was

eight years old. He

wore a baseball hat

and there were

patches on his

dungarees.

The middle-sized boy was six years old. He wore a sailor's hat and a bandage over each knee. He had fallen while learning to ride a two-wheel bike.

The littlest boy was three years old. He wore a cowboy hat and carried a pistol in one hand and a blanket in the other.

The eight-year-old boy said, "We want an old car."
The six-year-old boy said, "Yes, an old car. We
have a new car." The three-year-old boy said, "Old
car. Want an old car."
The eight-year-old explained to the garage man,
"Daddy uses the new car to go to work. We need

an old car for Mother to drive to the grocery store
and to take us to the library." The six-year-old
interrupted, "We need an old car to go see Grandma
when Daddy is at work."
The littlest one agreed, "Grandma. Go see Grandma."

The garage man pointed to Andrew and said,
"We have just the car for you—Andrew the automobile."

The boys' father raised Andrew's hood,
and he and the boys inspected the engine.
It was very long and had eight cylinders.
The garage man showed them the battery,
spark plugs, fan belt, radiator and horns.

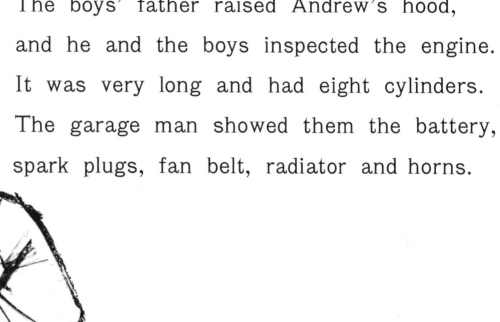

Inside the car they saw . . .

a clock to tell time,

a radio for listening to music

and news, and a heater for

keeping warm on cold days.

While their father checked the tires, the boys traced pictures in the dust that covered Andrew's fenders. And silver gray paint sparkled in the sunshine!

Their mother exclaimed,

"Why, there's nothing wrong with this car. All it needs is a bath!"

Their father told the garage man,

"This automobile is just what we need.
We want to buy it."

So they did.

The boys were very happy.

Their mother and father

were happy, too.

And they drove Andrew,
the automobile, out of the garage,

hucket-
a-bucket

down the street

to their own house.